CANDID LOVE

Book 2

"Alexandra's
LOVE & ROMANCE"™
Series

By

Denise Daniella Darcy

Published by
Durango Publishing Corp.®

Acclaim for Denise Daniella Darcy and *CANDID LOVE*

"You are going to love this book. I enjoyed reading it because of the characters and how they interact with each other. It feels real. It's an easy, short read and has some steamy scenes in it. I'd recommend it to anyone looking for a good book to sit down to and not get back up until it's done." – Tiffany LeBlanc

"I loved this book. Honestly the whole series is a great read. This book was hard for me to put down just like all the others in the series. DDD is a wonderful writer and I look forward to every book she writes." – Yvette Gynderfield

"Enjoyed this one and Love the series!!" – Martha Sheringham

"Another great story. Wonderful novel! I've been waiting for this next book in the series and it did not disappoint. I love Alex and her best friend Gabby. Can't wait for the next one." – Cheryl Brooks

"I am hooked on this series of love and romance. Denise Daniella Darcy has a talent for writing stories that allow the reader to tune out the world for a while and follow Alex (or Samantha in the first series) as she meets her different love interests. Believable, enjoyable and you get the feeling that you are right there with Alex feeling everything she does.

"Readers will be turning the pages to see what happens next to Alex. And I love the extra alternate ending that DDD wrote for each story. That is just a great bonus." – Vicky Black

"Probably the think I like most about the stories in Denise Daniella Darcy's Love and Romance series is that I often find myself thinking that I am one of the characters in the story. I start to feel as if I am there, right in the middle of the story, right inside the head of Alex or Samantha, feeling what they do and experiencing what they are experiencing. It is like DDD is sitting on my shoulder whispering into my ear, that is how close I sometimes feel to the characters.

"Another thing I really like about this series is the length. The stories are shorter and that allows me to read them

when I have time, in an evening, after work, or on the weekend. I am not a fan of the big volumes that take forever to get through. These stories have all that the long ones do, good characters, a great storyline, interesting dialogue, they just don't have that heaviness attached to them. For me they are the perfect length.

"And while I am mentioning what I like about this series, I have to say that the alternate endings that DDD writes is a novel (pun intended!) and creative way to keep the reader guessing. Even if you think you know what is going to happen, with the alternate ending, it is always a surprise.

"Great writing, great stories, great characters. I am definitely a big fan." – Judy St. Pierre

Also by Denise Daniella Darcy

Samantha's

LOVE & ROMANCE Series

First Love – Book 1

Rebound Love Book 2

Cowboy Love – Book 3

Casual Love – Book 4

FREE BONUS – ALTERNATE ENDINGS

Hi Readers, Denise here. I just wanted to let you know that I have an unexpected bonus for you. I have written an alternate ending for CANDID LOVE, and it is yours absolutely free.

Why, you may ask? Simple. I always strive to give more than the anticipated, more than the normal. The alternate ending dramatically changes the outcome and is interesting, unique and original.

Go here to access your FREE alternate ending:

http://www.denisedanielladarcy.com/CandidLoveAltEnding

Just my way of giving you something extra and thanking you for reading my books.

I am busy writing more stories in my Love and Romance series so check my website at http://www.DeniseDaniellaDarcy.com for the most up-to-date list. Or just get my FREE newsletter to stay on top of new developments. Available at: www.denisedanielladarcy.com/newsletter.

Happy reading -

Denise Daniella Darcy

PS. And as an added SPECIAL BONUS, at the end of this story I have attached a SNEAK PREVIEW of COMIC CON LOVE, Book 3 in the series. Enjoy!

FYI - The stories in Alexandra's LOVE & ROMANCE Series can be read in any order. The stories are linked but each one is a separate story. Research has shown that most readers do prefer to read them in sequence.

Other Titles By Durango Publishing Corp.®

Table of Contents

Chapter 1 -- Hawaiian hospitality

"Hawaiian Airlines welcomes you to Honolulu International Airport." The cheery voice of the flight attendant broke out over the public address system with an enthusiasm that Alex could barely stomach. She hated flying, always had, right from her first trip overseas with her family when she had spent the duration throwing up and suffering ear aches.

"The weather outside is a beautiful ninety degrees with the gorgeous Hawaiian sun shining down." Alex groaned softly and pressed her face into her hands, squeezing her palms against her eyes.

She really did not want to be this miserable, especially since she was just arriving in Hawaii for a one month, all expenses paid gig for one of the most respected modeling agencies in the world

AND she was getting paid for it. Alex sighed and pulled up the complimentary night mask provided by the airline and peeked out at the interior of the plane as it started descending toward the runway.

Tourists in oversized, colorful Hawaiian shirts, families, couples, a few businessmen, and senior citizens huddled together in excited tour groups whispering eagerly while pointing at glossy tourism brochures. Alex smiled to herself despite the dull throbbing in her head and the barely restrained nausea. Life wasn't so bad after all.

Alex had taken this assignment despite the fact that it had been 'arranged' by her father. She had a fiercely independent streak in her, ironically inherited from her father and she hated being handed things. There was a stubborn work ethic that touched all aspects of her life and caused her to work with Zen like dedication and focus.

That was also part of why she had landed the gig.

The modeling agency she had been contracted to was known for its strict professional standards, for everything from the models they hired right down to the lighting crew and spot boys. All in all it had been her talent and professionalism that had gotten her the job. Her father had only made the introductions, but still it rankled her a great deal.

Her thoughts were interrupted when the tires of the plane made contact with the tarmac and the plane skidded and screeched, but only for a brief second before resuming its speedy path and finally taxiing to a stop. The mass of passengers started trickling out of the plane doors in a steady dribble and before she knew it Alex was standing in the Hawaiian sun.

She closed her eyes for a moment and breathed in deeply; the air was warm and bright and smelt of the sea. She smiled again as she felt her nausea dissipating in the warm tropical sun. She gathered her single carry on, her bottle of water and her hat and headed towards the baggage claims area, rubbing shoulders with enthusiastic Japanese tourists, tired parents herding hyperactive children and all of the rest of the people that had come to experience Hawaii.

She was greeted first at the gate with flowery garlands draped over her neck by beautiful grass skirt wearing females and then at the baggage carousel by the terrifying mass of humanity she had just shared a flying metal tube with. The next few minutes were a blur of loud raucous sounds, bumping trolleys and scuffed luggage. Apparently she wasn't the only one who had been eager to get off the plane.

The exit gate had another welcome for her, in the form of a gorgeous tanned, dark haired, brown-eyed island boy waiting with the most stunning smile she had seen. Her heart skipped a beat when she noticed the sign he was holding, a simple piece of cardboard paper with her name on it. She couldn't help the smile that spread over her lips as she made her way over to him.

"Miss Alexandra?" he asked, the most adorable accent in his voice. "Aloha!" he responded to the wordless smile on Alex's face, draping his arms around her in a warm, welcoming hug and hoisting another garland around Alex's neck.

"Lemme get dose for you," he offered gallantly and took Alex's bags from her.

Alex, who had forgotten her ordeal of flying and was just grinning ear to ear, mooning at the perfect example of Hawaiian hospitality, 'Nope' she thought to herself, 'Not a hard gig at all.'

Chapter 2 -- Embarrassment and girlish delight

The inside of the car Alex stepped into was unlike anything she had seen before. Back in her hometown, cabs were a steady, uniformly decorated monolithic army of yellow and blue with one car completely identical to the next. What she was sitting inside, she could only describe as 'Inharmonious '.

There was a slew of feather boas and brightly colored drawing papers taped onto the walls in what she assumed was an attempt at decorating. Twin bobble headed luau girls wobbled their plastic necks on the dashboard of the car and the radio blasted Bob Marley unashamedly. If not for the glass divider between the driver and passenger, Alex would never have guessed that she was in a cab.

"So," she leaned forward and spoke loudly, trying to get herself heard over the sound of reggae music drifting out of the radio. "I'm Alex…" She offered tentatively and before she could react, he had turned around almost completely and stuck his hand through the window dividing the front and the back of the cab.

"Nico," he said happily, offering her his hand. "Pleased to meet you." Alex swallowed a small scream as Nico's turning around caused the cab to veer a little wildly on the road.

He drove as he decorated, unconventionally, unrestricted by norms or common sense and out of the lines. Alex's fingers clamped down onto the soft plush seat she was sitting on and she tried desperately not to sound like a complete dork.

"So…how long have you been driving a cab?" she asked trying to keep panic out of her voice as Nico barely managed to drive past an oncoming truck.

"Oh dis?" he looked down at the steering wheel he was so deftly managing to maneuver with just one hand. "Dis isn't my cab Alex," he grinned happily at the surprise on her face, "is my neighbors, just borrowing it to pick you up from the airport."

Another sharp swerve, another swallowed scream, Alex could feel her knuckles turning white. "So…uh…what's your neighbor doing today?" she asked trying to keep her mind off the escalating speedometer.

Nico shrugged at the question. "My gig down at the studio, jus' holding down t'ings you know?" He replied to her question as matter of fact, as if she had asked him what color the sky was.

He could sense the confusion in her look and glanced in the rear-view mirror to lock eyes with her. "Here we work different, yeah?" Alex couldn't help but smile at the utter simplicity and sincerity of his words.

She wondered how differently she would have to work now that she was here as well. "So you're not a cab driver, what are you?" She leaned forward, running her fingers through her hair trying to once again get herself heard over the sound of the radio.

Nico grinned into the rear-view mirror and Alex's heart thrilled at the twin little dimples that formed in his cheeks. "Whatever da lady wants." He shrugged with such a laid-back, confident gesture that Alex couldn't help but match the smile he offered her.

"I'm a photographer, what can you help me with?" she teased him lightly, her own hazel eyes twinkling with playfulness.

Nico chuckled softly. "Oh a photographer? I don't trust photographers." He teased her right back. "All dey wan' do is get me out of my clothes and take loads of pictures for dem girly magazines."

Alex cupped her laughter in her hands and blushed lightly at the playful flirtation. "Shucks! You caught me out!" she replied, her voice still tingling with laughter.

Nico responded with another dazzling smile of his. "Yeah, I'm a sharp customer see?" following up the words with a playful wink.

Alex smiled softly and shook her head. It seemed like ages since she had had good, old fashioned flirty fun with a guy, since she had allowed herself to, ever since Adam. She sighed at the memory and leaned back into her seat, continuing to gaze out the window in silence.

The silence didn't last long though as only a few moments later Nico announced that they had arrived at the small villa resort the agency was renting out for staff over the course of the month. Alex smiled and couldn't help appreciate the muscles that bulged beneath tribal tattoos on Nico's arms as he helped her with her luggage.

"See you tonight?" Nico asked as Alex pushed the last of her bags into her room.

"What?" Alex blinked at his words; did he just ask her out on a date? Did she miss the asking out?

Nico laughed at the perplexed expression on her face. "Take it easy eh?" he grinned teasingly. "I only meant the welcome party tonight."

He grinned as he leaned forward, "And besides… you only want me for my body."

Alex blushed heatedly at the light teasing before cupping her face in one hand and nodding. "Yes Nico, you'll see me tonight," before closing the door behind her and squeaking into her palms with that sweet mixture of embarrassment and girlish delight. She peeked out from one of the windows as she heard his cab drive out towards the road and smiled softly to herself.

So far Hawaii was turning out to be an excellent choice.

Chapter 3 -- Meeting the boss

The party that had been touted earlier as a 'meet and greet' turned out to be a full on red carpet, paparazzi and booze affair. Precisely the kind of arrangement that Alex had hoped to avoid, she nevertheless got herself dolled up appropriately.

She arrived at the resort dressed in a white, spaghetti strap summer dress. The fabric light and breezy danced over the tops of her thighs, the white of the fabric contrasting beautifully against her olive toned skin. She accessorized sparsely, adding only a pair of silver hoop earrings and a bangle on her left wrist. Her dark hair was pulled back in a strict ponytail. The overall effect one of elegant uncomplicated simplicity.

Apparently she was the only one who had gotten the memo. Everyone else was dressed in designer wear, little black dresses and stiletto pumps galore. She winced internally as she watched a pair of leggy blondes strut past her. Insecurity rushed up in her in a small panicky wave as she realized she was the only one not utterly and completely dolled up to the nines.

"Now this is typical Alex Luciano luck," she murmured self-deprecatingly as she made her way past the catwalk crowd and tried to blend in as best as she could.

She felt a hand against the small of her back five minutes into the party and she turned to the sight of her new friend. "Nico!" she felt the grin spread across her face a little too quickly, the color spreading on her cheeks to match the smile.

"In da flesh," he grinned that charming doubled dimpled smile back at her.

Alex bit her lip and smiled as she looked him up and down, eyebrow arched playfully. He had ditched the cargo shorts and bright red Hawaiian shirt for a classy white, double coat-tailed tuxedo. A red satin cummerbund across his waist. His dark hair, boyishly messy in the afternoon when she had seen him had been slicked back over his head and the red bow tie he was wearing emphasized his square jaw and chiseled chin.

"You clean up pretty good," Alex remarked with a smile on her lips, approvingly.

Nico looked down at himself and laughed softly. "Oh dis? Dis is a rental, got it from..."

Alex completed his sentence for him. "From your neighbor?"

Nico smiled wryly, rubbing at the back of his head with boyish charm. "From my boss actually."

"Your boss?" Alex tilted her head questioningly and Nico nodded. "A-yeah, he da one who own da business, throw da party and everyt'ing."

Alex blinked at that bit of information. "Wait a minute…you work for George Carlyle? Of the Carlyle media group?"

Nico scratched at his temple with one finger, seemingly surprised at that bit of information. "Mistuh Carlyle, yeah," he added finally, before thumbing in a direction behind him. "Da one with all dem models on him?"

Alex peeked over Nico's shoulder to peek at her employer. George Carlyle was something of a legend in the media industry. A complete outsider who had staked his own claim, a niche corner of the media world but fiercely defended and turned it into a respectable and profitable company. He was now set to move further into the industry, starting with the launch of his own modeling company. Which is where Alex came in.

She was one of several photographers hired to cover the launch and the model's portfolios. She had been hired through a third party and had never actually gotten to meet the man himself. To be frank, she was not relishing the opportunity. George Carlyle had a reputation for being an unforgiving taskmaster, a perfectionist who demanded the absolute best and more from his employees.

Alex, in fact, had heard the horror stories about the man before anything related to his professional acumen and what she had heard made her tummy squeeze nervously. Despite her outward professionalism she had a soft underbelly of anxiety and insecurity, something which required her to look for bosses that were flexible and understanding.

Candid Love

Even though she had never had need of their flexibility or understanding. She just needed to know the feeling of security, that safety net that allowed her to work freely.

Nico, of course, who shared none of Alex's concerns, cheerfully made his way over to where his employer was and discreetly whispered something into his ear. Alex watched in slight panic as Mr. Carlyle glanced over in her direction, nodded at Nico and began making his way over to her.

"Miss Luciano?" Alex swallowed softly at the sound of his voice. It was rich and deep and sounded like it would have been perfect behind the lead singer of a jazz band.

"Yes?" she replied far more mousy than she had hoped to.

"Welcome to the team." Alex looked down at the proffered hand before meekly meeting it with her grip.

Her new boss gave her slim hand a gentle squeeze, nodded and walked away without a single word and left Alex glaring daggers at Nico, who just shrugged with the most clueless smile on his lips.

Chapter 4 -- Moonlit walk

The rest of the evening was spent relatively comfortably, enjoyably even. Alex mingled with her soon to be subjects, got to know her fellow photographers and enjoyed the excellent food and drink available. The presence of the handsome Nico was a nice bonus as well. Actually it was the main reason why Alex felt so comfortable throughout the evening.

Any time the conversation got too boring, the party got too stifling, Nico would be by her side as if by magic. Whispering something in that accented voice of his, saying something utterly ridiculous and completely adorable at the same time or simply just offering his advice as to which food she should try. Thanks to Nico, Alex spent the better part of the evening smiling and enjoying the choicest dishes.

As the evening wore on and the party dwindled, Alex found herself lingering back more and more. She watched as the other photographers excused themselves to their rooms, the organizers left, some with the models. She even forced herself to stay back and listen to the drunken inane chatter of the models, quite a few of them well and truly sloshed.

It wasn't until the caterers started walking in and covering up the buffet and carrying out the chairs that Alex finally gave up. She was about to walk out of the resort when she heard the familiar lilted sound of Nico's voice.

"Going home? So soon?" Alex turned in the direction of the voice and had to laugh when she saw Nico.

He had undone the top button of his shirt, the red bow now hung limply from his neck, the jacket was slung carelessly over the railing of the stairs he was standing on and his feet were bare of shoes and socks with the bottoms folded up to his muscular calves.

"Yeah…it's kinda late," Alex replied with a grin on her lips and nodded in the direction of the cottages provided as residence for the staff.

"Yeah it is," Nico nodded in agreement before nodding in the direction of the beach that lay only a few steps away from them. "Best time for a walk though, yeah?"

Alex laughed softly and looked over in the direction of the beach before nipping at the corner of her bottom lip. She paused to reflect for a moment before smiling and nodding at Nico. "Alright, but a short walk," Alex said as she walked towards him, her steps graceful and feminine.

Nico nodded sagely at her words. "You're right, I have no idea what kind of wahine, what kind of woman, you might be."

Alex laughed softly and shook her head gently, one eyebrow arched playfully. "You can never be too careful you know."

Nico nodded back completely serious. "I know." The two shared a fleeting moment of silence before the night air echoed with their laughter.

Their moonlit walk along the beach was something straight out of a schoolgirl's romantic fantasy. They talked and laughed until their steps in the sand were accompanied by a warm, comfortable silence. Stars twinkled above them like shy fireflies peeking down curiously upon just the two of them. The ocean roared around them, a constant, almost hypnotic drone of the surf crashing upon the beach. Alex shuddered slightly against the cool night breeze and a moment later Nico's white jacket was around her shoulders.

They finally came to a stop at a jagged edge of the beach. The rocks lay scattered in a semi-crescent that collected the sea water in a sparkling, undisturbed pool. Alex gasped softly at the sight of the picture perfect setting. Stars sparkled their reflection in the water and little ripples floated in the mini-pond with every splash of the sea against the sand. Alex turned around to look at Nico and he had that stupidly adorable grin on his lips again.

"It's my favorite place on the beach," he shrugged casually and Alex had to resist leaning up and kissing him right then and there.

Chapter 5 -- Candid love

The two sat down facing the ocean; Alex hugged her legs and rested her chin on her knees. "It's so beautiful," she whispered softly, and Nico smiled at her, reached over and helped tuck a stray strand of her dark hair behind her ear.

"My Tutu…My grandmother used to bring me here…to pray." Nico looked away into the distance, a half smile on his lips as he dipped his feet into the small placid pool they were sitting by.

"And what about your parents?" Alex spoke up gently, half knowing the answer to that question already.

Nico smiled at her and shrugged that easy going shrug of his. "Never met 'em…Pa left before I was born and mama died a year after I was born." Alex bit down against her lip to keep from reacting to that bit of news. Her own mother's death flashed across her mind and the pain surged in her anew.

"Is alright." Nico smiled at her, sensing her unease even without her communicating it. "It was a good childhood, lotsa family, lotsa friends." He smiled softly at her. "Small island, means almost everyone is Ohana, is family." His words flowed with the casualness of an orphan who had learned how to mask his pain well. Alex knew the technique all too well.

"My mom died when I was young too," Alex whispered out the words gently, her eyes reflecting the pale moonlight. "I was twelve, it was a car accident." She smiled weakly at the look of intense empathy in Nico's gaze and wider still when his strong, tanned hands gently closed around her hands.

There was a silent moment of communication between two hurt souls before Nico's face changed and that wide, boyish grin returned to it. "Ai! Lookit!" he exclaimed happily before jumping feet first into the small pond, dress pants and all.

He waded out of it carrying a beautiful red orchid, the flower cupped tenderly in his hands. Alex laughed softly at the sight of him as he waded out of the pool, pants dripping water and Nico completely unperturbed.

"Is a Lehua blossom!" he exclaimed happily. "There is this Hawaiian legend about this flower. Want to hear it?"

"Yes, of course," Alex answered.

As Nico described the story, his eyes lit up with excitement. "The legend says that one day Pele, the goddess of the volcano, met a handsome warrior named Ohia and she asked him to marry her. Ohia, however, had already pledged his love to Lehua. Pele was furious when Ohia turned down her marriage proposal, so Pele used her magical powers to transform the young man into the ugly Ohia tree. Lehua was heartbroken, of course. The gods took pity on Lehua and decided it was an injustice to have Ohia and Lehua separated. So, they transformed Lehua into a lovely red blossom to adorn the Ohia tree so that the two lovers would be forever joined together. Now when anyone picks a Lehua blossom, it will rain because the lovers have been separated."

"Wow, that is bittersweet and tragic," Alex sighed.

Kneeling down by her side Nico offered the red blossom to her. Alex reached for the flower only to have Nico pull away and shake his head. "Nah! Not like that wahine!" he grinned, "Behind your ear, pretty lady."

Alex smiled and sat up straighter. "Which ear?" she grinned and lifted her bangs up playfully.

Nico chuckled and explained, "Well...left ear if you already have a mate...right if you are looking for one."

Alex smiled shyly, a pinkish blush coloring her cheeks as she tucked her bangs behind her right ear, turning sideways to Nico to offer him the space. Nico's grin widened even as he tried not to let it show. He leaned forward, gently tucking the orchid behind her ear and as he did so Alex turned her head ever so slightly towards him.

Before they knew the space between their lips had disappeared. Alex felt her heart skip in her chest as their heated breaths mingled together for a moment, the softness of their mouths pressed against each other in a slow molten dance.

Nico broke the kiss gently and leaned back to look down into Alex's gaze, questioning silently. Alex replied with a smile, her hands gently slid up over the front of his muscled shoulders before she leaned up on her toes and pressed her lips back against Nico's.

Time seized around them as they melded together in their embrace. Alex murmured an incoherent thought into their kiss as her lips parted for the wet caress of Nico's tongue. Nico slipped his arm around Alex's waist, one hand slid down to cup against the soft tight curve of her bottom and squeezed gently before lifting her up gently onto his lap.

Alex bit down on a small mischievous grin as she pressed herself down against the telltale bulge in the front of Nico's pants. The husky moan that he whispered against Alex's throat let her know how much he appreciated that gesture.

It was Alex's turn to whimper as she felt Nico's hands move up over the shapely softness of her thighs, boldly pushing her dress up over her legs until it was bunched up over her waist. Her words breathed gently against his skin as his thumbs hooked in the waistband of her panties and slowly began to peel them off.

"So, I'm that kind of wahine now?" she whispered playfully against his lips and Nico responded with a boyish grin on his lips.

"You are that kind of wahine," Nico breathed softly before gently covering the sound of Alex's reply with his lips.

Alex moaned into the kiss, the warmth of his breath mingled with hers even as his hand slipped between her legs to caress against the wetness of Alex's arousal. Nico's fingers strummed against her slick, swollen lips. Alex broke the kiss briefly to groan a husky growl as Nico fingered her, his wrist grinding forward and up into her, making her muscles tense against the rhythmic motion of his digits inside her, making her thighs shiver with the strain of her own lust and need.

"Please…" Alex whispered, lips brushing carelessly against her lovers mouth. "I need it," the sound of her own voice, of her own words stoked her arousal even more.

She felt Nico's chest rumble with a slow hungry growl as he cupped Alex's ass firmly in one hand, lifting her up effortlessly. Alex had only a moment to realize what was going on before she felt Nico's throbbing cock press up against the wet eager slit of her pussy and a moment later her eyes rolled into the back of her head as she sank herself down on his swollen member.

Alex bit back a hungry moan as she sank herself further down on Nico's fat cock. Her hands rested on his shoulders as his slipped further up her form, raising the fabric up over her bra less breasts, up over her head and abandoning it on the sea splattered rock.

Nico's mouth wrapped around a pebbled brown nipple as Alex began rocking in his lap. The sounds of their arousal were drowned out by the roar of the surf.

Nico leaned up and pressed his lips to Alex's once again, their kiss frantically passionate, unashamedly lustful. Alex began to grind herself forward on Nico, greedily pressing herself down onto him, feeling his impressive girth stretch her almost to the point of discomfort. Nico's hands cupped possessively over her firm buttocks and pulled her down harder, faster until he could feel the involuntary spasms start to ripple along his shaft.

Candid Love

Nico growled hungrily like a predator smelling blood and leaned forward to sink his teeth into the softness of Alex's throat. The soft throb of her pulse twitched against his lips as he rammed himself up into her completely and felt her clench tightly onto his cock.

"Oh god!" Alex moaned before gripping onto Nico, arms wrapped tightly around his frame as her orgasm ripped through her, mingled with that of Nico's and left her utterly bereft of words to express her emotions.

The silence afterwards was warm and intimate, starlit and peppered with the smell of sea salt. It was the silence of intimacy, of passion sated and kindled at the same time. Alex was the first one to break it, her voice breathless and gentle.

"I don't usually do this," Alex tried whispering a bashful explanation but Nico cut it off with an adamant yet affectionate kiss.

"Maybe you should start doing more of it?" He chuckled at the light swat at his shoulder before wrapping his arms around her and smiling into the warm embrace of her scent, her warmth, her laughter, the night sky seeming to wrap around the two lovers as they held onto each other in the darkness.

Chapter 6 -- Sharp cheekbones and confrontational demeanor

"Alright people! Lunch break!" The voice of the studio director rang out through the crackled sound of his bull horn, over the muted buzz that was the collective sound of about a dozen models, photographers and studio staff collected together.

Alex let out a soft sound of relief, her palm pressed against her forehead as she took a moment to just breathe. The first day of work had been the equivalent of a Spanish bull run. She had barely been avoiding getting trampled all day long. Operative word being 'barely'.

The day had started off with her accidentally spilling her coffee over one of the aspiring models to be. A platinum blonde with cheekbones that looked like they could cut glass. The incident had of course spiraled into a massive drama fest with the model throwing the grown-up equivalent of a tantrum. The model's agents getting involved and finally Alex had to be shifted to another part of the studio to get away from the histrionics of the leggy blonde.

The other end of the studio hadn't been much better either. The setup of the shoot was such that there were partitions or photography areas set up wherein each photographer had a personalized and thematic space to shoot his or her model. So in effect there were twelve of these cells set up in a wide circular ring with photographers constantly clicking away. The effect was one of magnificent chaos and hectic energy. It was nothing like anything Alex had ever seen before.

Alex caught a break with the model, a Hawaiian native born to a Japanese mother and a local father. She was absolutely stunning and utterly exotic. If Alex had to put a face to Hawaii she would choose Nani's without question. The two had bonded almost instantly. It was Nani's first time working for such a prestigious company and she was just as nervous as Alex working for Mr. Carlyle. The photo shoot was a combination of nervous energy, warm laughter and the hectic exhaustion of a job utterly well done.

"Wanna grab some lunch?" Alex looked up at the sound of Nani's voice and realized she had been in some faraway place. "My treat" Nani offered.

Alex smiled and nodded, "Sure." She put her camera in her bag and strapped the bag across her chest as she got up with Nani to walk towards the food stalls set up at the far end of the studio.

Nani was dressed in a brilliant green bikini with flowers dotting the skimpy material. Her dark chocolate skin tone matched perfectly with the color of her bikini, as well as the color of her eyes. Alex was wearing her favorite pair of mom jeans, converse sneakers and a faded gray tank top that looked like it would look good on a greasy mechanic, topped off with a ratty denim baseball cap. The two looked as different as east and west and yet they were drawn to each other like peanut butter and jelly.

Nani introduced Alex to Hawaiian made pork sandwiches and Alex promised Nani her firstborn after taking only the first bite of the treat. They spent their allotted time sitting together and chatting and laughing while the rest of the models spent theirs getting touched up and munching on celery.

"Wow," Nani said through a mouthful of giggles and cider. "I am SO glad I met you, you have no idea how nervous I was."

Candid Love

Alex smiled warmly at the compliment and shrugged, "I'm really glad I met you too." Alex sighed as she leaned back in her chair, taking another sip of her cola. "You cannot believe how bitchy those models can be."

"Oh we aren't all that bad." Alex whipped her head around at the cold sound of the remark.

"Oh," Alex squeaked softly at the sight of the blonde she had offended this morning, she of the sharp cheekbones and confrontational demeanor.

Of course this time she had another two of her clique with her, an almost identical but slightly shorter blonde and a dark haired buxom Latina. Alex suddenly had a flashback of high school trauma and couldn't help but crack a smile at the collected trio. The gesture only seemed to irritate the head blonde further.

"The fuck are you smiling about skank?" she snarled angrily at Alex, her slender fingers curling into tight fists.

"Nothing! Nothing!" Alex hastily sputtered, raising her hands in neutrality. She really did not want to set off another incident, especially on her first day.

"Why don't you just leave us alone?" All four of them turned in astonishment towards Nani, the newbie, the youngster who had just dared stand up to queen bee herself.

Cheekbones glared in shock at the outburst of the young one before her lips curled upwards in a menacing grin. "Oh you have no idea what I am going to do to you." Her voice was icy cold and it was matched in intensity by the cool of the second voice that spoke out.

"Yes, what ARE you going to do to her?" This time all five of them turned in surprise to see their employer standing over them.

Chapter 7 -- Charmed

Mr. Carlyle had appeared as if out of thin air and now stood silently glaring down at them. Effortless in the dominance and power that he exuded and subtle in the suggestion of complete and utter control. There was something about his eyes that reminded Alex of this beautiful photograph that her father had snapped somewhere in the Amazon. That of a beautiful, sleek Jaguar hidden behind the leaves of the heavy foliage.

Those green eyes held the exquisite mystique of knowledge and complete control. The exact same look was shared by Mr. Carlyle as he cast his gaze over each of the five girls present there. Cheekbones spoke first.

"Mr. Carlyle!" Her voice had lost all venom and had been replaced with warm dripping honey, the pout of her silicone enhanced lips didn't hurt either. "We were just asking the new girl to come join us on the patio."

She innocently pointed towards the raised platform a few meters away where the rest of the models were milling about grazing on salads. Mr. Carlyle turned his head slightly looking in the direction of the platform and then back at cheekbones.

"I will be keeping them company, thank you Carla." Alex couldn't help but shudder at the subtle strength in the tone of his voice. It sounded like thunder wrapped in silk and Carla cheekbones wilted meekly away from him.

"Yessir," she muttered under her breath as she and her lackeys slunk away, though not before shooting Alex a dirty, hateful look.

Alex in turn just sighed in relief. A small part of her felt betrayed at the lack of confrontation but it was accompanied by a much bigger part of her that felt relieved all the same. She turned to look at Mr. Carlyle who seemed to be watching her with a mixture of amusement and curiosity.

"Thank you," she gushed, despite not wanting to. "I really didn't like the direction that conversation was going."

Mr. Carlyle turned to her with that mixture of amusement and mild disdain, as if she were some amusing new contraption on a toy shelf. "And what direction was that exactly?"

Alex felt another shudder run up her spine at the sound of that rich, deep voice of his and his gaze on her made her fumble over her words much more clumsily than usual. "You know..." she shrugged helplessly, "the bullying direction?"

Thankfully Nani stepped in before she could say something even more awkward. "Mr. Carlyle," she spoke up pleasantly, confidently, displaying far more panache than her twenty-one years would have led Alex to believe, "I'm Nani."

Mr. Carlyle took one look at the slender, tanned hand before enveloping it in his own large, powerful, surprisingly calloused hand. "Charmed." The word was spoken with old school elegance and manliness. The kind that conjured up images of men in fedoras and trench coats and old amber colored scotch.

"So...Nani, how are you finding the facilities?" Alex had to blink at the ease with which Mr. Carlyle made the transition from hardened boss to smooth charmer. The hardness of his voice melting from steel to satin.

"Apart from the...uh...company?" Nani grinned nodding towards the trio of models walking away from them. "I'd have to say this is pretty cool."

Mr. Carlyle laughed a deep throaty laugh, one that seemed utterly out of place against the backdrop of his seriousness. "Well I'm very glad about that Nani, please do let me know if there is anything I can do to add to the 'cool'" He offered Nani his personal card, the same old school charm coming as easily to him as breathing.

"Thank you, I will," Nani added, her brown eyes almost twinkling as she palmed the card in her hands. "Now if you'll excuse me?" she asked him with that subtle hint of grace and confidence which Alex was already jealous of.

"Of course," Mr. Carlyle nodded and smiled. It was almost a dance, Alex mused to herself, the simple elegant back and forth that lacked so sorely in modern conversations.

Alex was lost in her thoughts until she realized she was all alone with her employer. Nani had already walked away and Alex was left gawking at her six foot three boss.

"Miss Luciano?" Alex snapped out of her musings at the sound of his voice.

"Uh...yeah? I mean...yes?" she sputtered nervously.

"Will you join me for drinks tonight?" he asked her in the most casually simple of ways as if asking about the weather.

"Of course," Alex replied mechanically, not really thinking about her answer and it wasn't until Mr. Carlyle had walked away that she realized she had been asked out by and agreed to go out with her boss.

"Fuck," she groaned under her breath.

Chapter 8 -- A date?

Alex squirmed in place as she sat on the stool in the fancy bar. Her 'date' with her boss was about to officially start in fifteen minutes and Alex had arrived nearly forty minutes ago. The time spent in taking in the surroundings had done nothing to assuage her frayed nerves. On the contrary, since arriving she had found her stress levels increased and tightened.

The bar was attached to the hotel her boss was staying in. A five star, luxury hotel the likes of which Alex had dreamed of visiting, but not like this. Her fingers rotated the empty glass, long drained of her club soda, the glass still cool and slick to the touch. She sighed as she checked her wrist watch for the third time in the past five minutes.

The slender silver chain of the watch slid over her wrist as she put her arm back down. Father time was being a real asshole. Alex ran her fingertip over the wet rim of her glass and thought about what she was doing in this bar. Was she really on a date with her boss? Was it really what she thought it was? She bit down on her bottom lip considering the repercussions of her actions.

Her thoughts were left unfinished however at the sound of that now familiar deep bass voice. "Miss Luciano?"

Alex shifted on her seat, swiveling it almost to the point of spinning right off it. Her heels clacked on the floor as she stood up with almost a snap. "Mr. Carlyle!" her voice betrayed the surprise she felt.

Mr. Carlyle looked at her with an amused smile before checking his watch. "Am I late?"

Alex tittered nervously "Oh…no…not at all…sir!" The sound of her voice cracked nervously as she bit down on her lip and looked over her shoulder as if expecting any one of her peers to be standing there, looking on disapprovingly.

"Miss Luciano?" Alex turned at the sound of her boss's voice. His dark brown eyes were looking down at her with a mixture of concern and amusement. "Are you alright?"

Alex looked down at her feet and then back into those amazing eyes. "No…no, I'm not," her words were accompanied with a heavy sigh.

She reached for her purse, pulling it off the bar counter easily. "Look Mr. Carlyle, I'm really flattered but I can't do this I'm sorry."

Her words tumbled out of her lips hastily, almost as if she didn't trust them to leave her lips afterwards. She glanced up at him once, afraid she had offended him, but far from being angry, Mr. Carlyle was cupping his hand against his mouth watching her with that same amused twinkle in his eyes.

"Miss Luciano," he began, his voice tinged with the sound of a smile. "What exactly do you think we are doing here?"

Alex paused at that and hesitated, she looked over her shoulder for her fictional colleague one more time before she spoke softly, timidly. "We're on a date?"

There was a brief pause in the conversation. Alex's ears rang with a high pitched sound in the aftermath of the silence. The sound exaggerated by the distant dull background jazz music that flowed easily in the bar.

"Hahahahahahaha." Alex blinked at the sound of his laughter, she took a step backwards in surprise and just watched as the man who was supposed to be, 'the new Caesar,' laugh himself to tears.

Alex could only glare at him for a few moments before she coughed and cleared her throat tersely. It wasn't that he was laughing at her; it was just that he seemed to be having so much fun without her. Mr. Carlyle glimpsed at her and cleared his throat; he wiped at the corner of his eyes lightly and spoke with a voice that was so utterly different than the steely growl he had used earlier at the photo shoot.

"Oh, I'm sorry Miss Luciano, it's just that…I called you here to discuss your work." He grinned brightly at her after the declaration and it took a few moments for Alex to realize that the heat radiating around her was from the blush on her own face.

"Oh my God," she whimpered under her breath, the color bright on her face. "I'm sorry…I didn't mean to assume…I mean….you…uh."

Mr. Carlyle grinned once again, a bright impish expression this time. "So wait…wait….you thought I asked you out on a date...and you came?"

Alex sputtered some more at his observation. "I…you know…uh…" She hung her head in defeat finally and sighed. "I wasn't gonna stay" she added finally, as a last despondent measure of defeat.

Mr. Carlyle smiled at her once more, this time genuine and warm. "Call me George," he said warmly as he offered Alex her purse, the one she had dropped in panic.

"Only if you call me Alex," her words were spoken through a meek, mousy grin and all of a sudden she didn't feel so awkward.

Chapter 9 --The boss man

After the initial embarrassment, Alex quickly found herself being drawn to her new boss. The two sat together outside on the balcony, a spot apparently reserved only for VIP guests. The cool night air blew against them tinged with the salt of the sea and the flavor of smoked bacon being prepared downstairs.

The stars pricked the darkness of the night above them in lieu of the moon's light and whatever dim darkness was left was dissipated by the lovely Chinese lanterns that hung out over the VIP area. All in all, Alex had to approve of the choice of location and the ambience. It was relaxed and comfortable and yet fancy and glamorous at the same time.

The two of them spent their time outside on the balcony without any interruption, except for a few other couples that enjoyed the beautiful night in the same comfortable silence. Alex was surprised with herself. Not only was she enjoying the company of an authority figure but she found herself gradually charmed by him as well. Something she had not expected.

George told her about his life history. Born to a couple of small town farmers in idyllic Kentucky, he left home at the age of sixteen with falsified documents to enlist in the marines and had seen enough of the world to realize what he really wanted to do. His life had turned towards photography with the help of his wife, his high school sweetheart.

Alex couldn't help but notice the subtle changes in the man as he spoke of his one true love. His eyes sparkled lightly and the corners of his lips rose and fell in slight, hidden smiles that would have gone unnoticed if Alex were not staring so intently at his face. She paused for a moment to look into George's eyes as he spoke about the heartbreak he had to face after his wife's death and Alex realized that the conversation had gone from professional to personal.

"I am so sorry to hear that," Alex said with genuine sympathy in her voice. George reacted with a half shrug that Alex had seen her father make so many times before.

"It's alright," he replied, with that same half smile, his eyes reflecting the sadness that he did not allow to surface in his words. "We had a good run." He turned away from her to look up towards the moonless, star-studded sky.

Alex followed his gaze up to the sky and let the cool, comfortable silence wrap around them before breaking it. "What happened?" She wasn't sure if she should be asking him this, but somehow felt compelled to.

"Accident," George replied quietly, the single word heavy with a thousand hidden nuances.

"I'm really sorry," Alex repeated, turning her gaze away from him and down at her feet which were pointed inwards towards each other awkwardly.

"I was driving," the words came out laden with grief, even though there was no change in his tone or pitch, "it was...we were coming back from getting the sonogram." Alex felt her heart sink at that revelation. They were coming back from getting a sonogram, she was pregnant.

"Oh God!" Alex gasped softly under her breath. Her hand slid over and gently grasped George's without even thinking about it. George turned his head towards her and smiled the saddest smile that Alex had ever seen in her life.

"I guess you can't really blame anyone for stuff like this." His words were strong and brave but the pain and anguish in his eyes could not be hidden even if he tried. "Anyways," George continued with another shrug, "after that…I decided I wanted to spend my life doing what Hannah wanted me to do." He smiled again at Alex. "She was a photographer too, she wanted me to stop being a wage slave and start my own business and so I did."

Alex smiled at that last bit. "So that's why you're such a hard-ass?" George blinked at those words and then laughed again, an unexpected, genuine and deep laugh that made his entire body shake. Alex grinned at that reaction. It made her feel good to bring joy to this complicated, hurt, wonderful man.

"Yeah I guess so," he said, his words still ringing with laughter. "It's not just a business for me, my work is my legacy." He paused and turned to her with a knowing smile on his lips. "Just like yours is."

Alex blinked at those words. "What do you mean?" she asked with raised eyebrows.

"Your work," George continued, "it's what you want to be your legacy, or rather it is your father's legacy that you carry on." Alex felt the slow realization kick in.

She didn't do this work for any other reason as powerful as that of her own father's legacy. She was a photographer because it was the one way of getting closer to her own father. "I…" she stuttered silently as she looked up at George who was now leaning towards her.

      "Don't worry," he whispered softly, "I won't tell," and that is when she kissed her boss.

Chapter 10 -- A confession

"Oh my God!" Alex whispered the words out with a mixture of incredulity and excitement. George smiled at her and nodded.

"My feelings exactly." He said the words through a smile and leaned forward to repeat the kiss only to feel Alex's hand on his shoulder.

"No! No, I meant we shouldn't do that, that wasn't right!" Her voice was breathless, she felt breathless and excited and scared.

George just laughed this time, a sound rich and heartfelt and something that Alex felt he didn't do often enough. "Oh well, if you insist on re-trying..." He grinned and leaned forward again, this time pressing his lips insistently against Alex's lips.

Candid Love

Alex responded with a nervous giggle, she really should not be doing this but there was something about the whole scenario which was so completely unlike her. Here she was on the veranda of an expensive restaurant making out with her boss, of all people. Something which she knew was an utterly bad idea but somehow seemed completely irresistible at the same time.

"Stop," she whispered softly against George's lips with a wavering uncertainty. Despite the whispered request she didn't move away from the comfort of George's caress and he picked up on that.

"Look," he said gently, his strong large hands cupping her suddenly trembling hands. "I'm going to try that again, and if you tell me to stop again…I will."

Alex looked up at him and grasped her bottom lip between her teeth. She wasn't sure she had the willpower to do what she should do but nodded anyway. George smiled and shifted in his seat, turning towards her completely and leaned forward. One hand cupped the side of Alex's face and the other held her hand tenderly. The kiss was soft and sumptuous at the same time, a thing of warmth and moist tenderness that made Alex squirm in her seat.

She didn't realize how long the kiss lasted, or cared, but when George withdrew from it, she hadn't asked him to stop. "This is such a bad idea," she sighed softly, a grin on her lips as she turned her face up towards him for more of the same. Good sense and appropriate behavior be damned.

Her heart raced in her chest as she pressed into the kiss eagerly, her lips parting softly for his warmth. Alex shifted slightly, turning towards the older man she was making out with. One hand came up to cup the slightly scrubby, wrinkled cheek of his face in her hand. A soft giggle bubbled up from her lips as she felt George's teeth lightly nip at her bottom lip.

Alex hadn't felt this excited to be making out with someone ever since her first time in high school and that had been far too many years ago to remember. This was a delicious combination of taboo, forbidden fruit and sensual experience. This was a bad idea and a good idea at the same time. Her thoughts were abruptly interrupted as she felt his hand slide between her legs.

"Oh my!" Alex gasped softly, the kiss broken on a heated breath as she caressed his face with one hand and bit down on her bottom lip. George smiled at the words and pecked at them on her lips. "You're not saying no anymore," he whispered and Alex had to laugh softly.

"Would you believe me if I did?" she asked even as she felt her thighs part, allowing him more access. George grinned and nuzzled lightly against her cheek. "Not a chance."

Alex laughed softly before her lips were pressed up against his once again and she shifted forwards. A moan vanished against the insistent press of George's lips as Alex wound her arms around his neck and pressed closer to him. He in turn slipped his hand up against the back of her neck, cupping her face tighter against him.

"Mmmm," Alex whimpered lustily, George's hand pressed tighter between her legs, expertly massaging against her excited, soaked sex.

"I have a confession to make," George whispered through heated breaths. "I didn't ask you here to talk about your portfolio." There was a lusty darkness to his voice that made Alex shiver with pleasure. His hand pushed forwards squeezing shamelessly, effortlessly against the now soaked mound of Alex's pantied sex.

"Unh!" Alex moaned, her lips parting on an unfinished sound of pleasure before they curved upwards in a wicked, unabashedly hungry smile. "You don't say."

Alex leaned forward to press herself into another extended session of heavy petting and warm, silken kisses when she heard her name exclaimed by someone other than George.

"Alex?" She turned around at the sound to see a recently familiar figure standing in the doorway of the veranda. "Nico?!" She gulped softly. She couldn't see his face completely in the darkness but there was no mistaking the hurt in his voice.

Chapter 11 -- Comfort from home

"Pop?" The word was breathed over the sound of soft crackling static that usually accompanied international phone calls. "I know you're probably sleeping, I just wanted to let you know," Alex hesitated for a moment. What exactly did she want her father to know? That she missed him? That she wished he was awake to answer her questions? That she felt like absolute crap for the way she had behaved over the past few days?

She sighed softly and took a deep breath. "Just call me when you can OK? Love you." She hung up the phone with a heavier heart than before. There was a moment of cricket chirped silence before she shifted her weight and rolled onto her side on the bed. The single table lamp on the bedside table was the only source of illumination in the room. That and the bright fluorescent glow of her mobile screen.

Candid Love

Alex brushed her thumb across the screen of the phone and scrolled down the list of the phone numbers she had called. The last one had been to her dad, the other fifteen had been to Nico. She rolled over onto her stomach and muffled a groan into the soft pillow. She wanted so very desperately to call him to let him know that what he had seen, what he had heard, was not what he thought.

Well, actually, it was what he thought, her making out with her boss while at the same time leading on another man. What she really wanted to do was to let him know that she was not that person, that it was only a momentary loss of judgment, that she really liked him and the last thing she wanted to do was hurt him. Now if only he would pick up her call, any one of them.

Alex chewed lightly on her bottom lip before she reached for her phone again. Her hand hesitated for a moment as it hovered over the bright screen of her phone, thumb trembling. She sighed and put the phone back down, leaning her head back against her pillow again. Her eyes closed for a moment, tightly, firmly before she reopened them and sat up again. There was another moment of uncertainty before she swiped her thumb over her phone's screen and pressed it down against the one number she felt so conflicted about calling.

"Hello?" a sultry, sleepy voice answered on just the second ring.

Alex smiled at the sound of her best friend's voice. "Gabby?" There was a moment's pause followed by the rustling of sheets and the hint of whispers from another voice and Alex immediately regretted calling her. Gabby wasn't alone.

"Alex," Gabby cleared her voice from the other side of the line, "Alex is everything OK?"

Candid Love

Alex felt like crying at the sound of the familiarity in Gabby's voice. It had been far too long since the two friends had spoken, and to Alex the duration now seemed like an eternity.

"Oh Gabby," Alex whispered, as she clutched the phone tightly in her grip. "Oh Gabby, I did something so stupid," and that was that, the past was washed away in just a few moments of their first contact together.

Alex stayed up talking and Gabby stayed up a few thousand miles away listening. Alex sank deeper, tighter into the comforting softness of her bed while Gabby slipped out of hers and walked around barefoot in her apartment making coffee and listening to her best friend spill her heart out.

Words preceded tears, tears came before reconciliation and reconciliation was followed by choked, hesitant laughter and the comforting warmth that comes only when two best friends talk through the night. Gabby refused to let Alex be miserable, it was just that simple, no matter how badly Alex tried to beat herself up Gabby simply refused it to be so. It was late into the night when Alex finally started getting a grip on herself, when she finally managed to stop the panicked descent into desperation.

"I missed this." It was Gabby who spoke first, who voiced the words that Alex was thinking.

"I missed this too," Alex replied, a smile on her lips.

It felt really good to have her back, past indiscretions and all. "We should do more of this when you get back," Gabby said, her voice sounding distant and far away and so close by at the same time.

"Deal!" Alex smiled into her words as she closed her eyes and listened to Gabby talk from the other side of the phone, from a world away.

Morning came far too early for Alex, and far too late for sleep. The natural beauty of the Hawaiian sunrise was made harsh by the lack of any rest for Alex. She groaned out against the bed sheets and rolled onto her side, turning her back to the sunlight in futile protest. She did not want to get out of bed, she wanted to call in sick and spend the day in darkness and despair. Unfortunately for her, this was a special assignment which meant no off days, no personal days, not even sick days. The fact was driven home by the shrill sound of her mobile phone going off inches from her ear.

"Alex?" the unwelcome sound rang over the phone. "Where the hell are you?" Alex groaned and rubbed at her temple with one hand trying to drown out the throbbing rebellion of her body against waking up.

"Who's this?" Alex groaned into the phone, barely recognizing the gravely rasp of her voice even as it issued from her lips.

"It's Nani, Alex" The name sounded familiar, the voice sounded familiar, where had Alex heard it before.

"Oh shit!" Alex exclaimed suddenly, wakefulness snapping her eyes open.

"'Oh shit' is right, where the hell are you? The shoot started over an hour ago" Alex glanced at the small clock by her bedside and groaned loudly as she staggered to her feet and began collecting her clothes.

"I'm leaving, I'm leaving!" Alex exclaimed into the phone even as she hopped on one foot towards the front door, trying to pull a shoe over the other foot. "Listen Nani, you have to…" Her words were cut off when the door opened on its own to reveal Nico standing there.

"Alex?" Nani's voice queried over the phone. "Alex are you there? I have to what?"

"I'll call you back," Alex murmured into the phone as she looked up at Nico, her heart in her throat, racked by mixed feelings of affection and guilt and relief and anxiety.

"I tried calling you," Alex spoke flatly, even though the expression in her eyes betrayed her emotions.

"I know," Nico replied, "fifteen times." Alex smiled at that, her gaze dropped to her feet and then back to that handsome face that made her belly ache.

"So," Nico stepped inside the room and closed the door behind him, "let's talk."

Chapter 12 -- A personal day

"I," Alex began, and then immediately bit down on her bottom lip. "I just...I want you to know that what you saw last night...it wasn't what you thought it was."

"Really?" Nico replied icily. "Because it looked like you making out with your boss."

Alex sighed and rubbed at the bridge of her nose as she walked back into the apartment, wearing only one shoe on her foot. "Look...I mean...that wasn't ...you know...that wasn't me trying to hurt you or play you."

She looked up at Nico, trying to find the warmth that she found there so easily. It wasn't there this time. "Nico...I...I'm not that kind of girl," her voice wavered a little as she searched his gaze.

"I don't know what kind of girl you are Alex," Nico shrugged lightly, large shoulders heaved up and down.

"What's that supposed to mean?" A note of ice crept into Alex's voice as well and her lips pressed together tightly against each other as she crossed her arms across her chest.

"I mean," Nico continued, turning his back towards her and casually strolling across the room, past her to look out the window. "I don't know what kind of girl you are, I don't know what you want, I don't know what you are doing here, or what you want…from me."

Her gaze followed his movements through the room. There was something very restrained about him here today. None of his usual exuberance, nothing of his incredible warmth and sweetness. This was him holding himself back.

"So then why are you here?" Alex asked him softly. "Nico?" She stepped forward towards him when he didn't reply, one hand squeezed against his shoulder gently. "Why?"

He stiffened slightly at her touch and straightened, the tautness of his muscles against her touch sent a thrill down Alex's spine and she couldn't resist the desire to lean against him.

"I'm here," he turned to face her, as he pressed one palm against her face and leaned forward, "for this." His whispered words pressed against Alex's lips before they were covered in the warmth of his kiss and Alex found herself melting against him.

"Wait," Alex whispered against his lips as she reached down with trembling fingers to grasp at the soft, flimsy fabric of her tank top. His fingers beat her to it and a moment later the fabric was yanked up over her head.

Alex laughed softly, a soft, flirtatious musical sound that made Nico smile and growl at the same time. He reached down and wrapped his arms around Alex's frame, lifting her up effortlessly. Alex responded by coiling her arms around his neck and her legs around his waist. She shuddered at the sensation of her bare breasts pressing against Nico's chest.

There was something so utterly sexy about a man this strong, this powerful who still treated you this delicately, this gently. Alex moaned at the press of his strong arms, at the gentle way that he squeezed the breath out from her, and at that incredible strength of his so carefully tempered with his gentleness.

Nico's mouth found Alex's once again and their kiss melted their breath together in a soft, wet passion of thrusting, coiling tongues. Alex reached down between the crushed spaces of their bodies and frantically grasped at Nico's belt buckle. The sound of metal clinking against marble signaled the dropping of Nico's pants and Alex moaned a second time as Nico reciprocated Alex's gesture by peeling her shorts off her.

Alex panted softly, her lips closed around Nico's earlobe as he leaned down and laid her on her back, his own frame pressing down against her in a slow grinding motion. Alex bit down on her lip and all of a sudden flashbacks to hormone fueled make out sessions flashed in her mind. She had to bite against Nico's jawline to stop herself from giggling.

Nico smiled and nuzzled against her cheek, his hands slid up over her slim arms and pinned her down by her wrists. "You t'inking this is funny huh?" he grinned over her, his lips curved upwards in a hungry, dangerous smile. "T'ink I'm funny?" he chuckled as he squeezed her wrists and pressed forward. The heated throb of his cock against her thigh made her arch up in almost feline lust. Nico smirked at her reaction and shifted his weight, pressing himself up against her, letting the underside of his thick cock grind up into the welcoming wetness of her pussy.

"Oh God!" Alex whimpered against the crook of Nico's neck as she spread her thighs further apart. There was a delicious depravity to this act of theirs. A surreal sensuality as she looked up into his eyes and moaned his name, felt him sink halfway into her, pause and then push forwards, sliding deep into her very core.

"NICO!" she shrieked softly, her arms curled tightly around his strong neck, finger nails digging into the flesh of his back. He responded by driving his hips forward hard enough to make the bed creak.

Alex felt the breath from her lungs escape in a single lusty moan, her eyes rolled into the back of her head as she gave herself over completely to him. Her nostrils flared in unabashed lust as she wrapped her legs, wrapped herself around Nico's form. Her ankles locked together and it was all she could do to keep from exploding with lust, to keep from losing herself.

Nico growled something incoherent against her ear and Alex shuddered from it. She carved her mark onto his very flesh with the cruel sharpness of her fingernails and Nico nibbled his along the soft, warm skin of her neck.

Alex closed her eyes and gave herself over to the primal, hungry sensation of being taken like this, of being mated with. The sound of the waves crashing against the shore combined with that of their panting breaths, creaking bed and the scent of their bodies writhing together.

"Fuck!" Nico groaned and Alex recognized the spiraling lust in that exclamation, she pressed her lips to his and clamped down even tighter on him. Demanding his pleasure, taking it just as he took hers.

"Oh fuck!" This time it was Alex who groaned, louder, higher pitched and more desperate. Her voice shook and her gaze locked with her lover's as they both tumbled off the edge of their pleasure together.

It was a long time before either of them spoke. They were content to be tangled with each other like this, to be bonded together like this and for a moment it was all there was.

Alex smiled softly as Nico raised his head and leaned forward to press a kiss to her chin. "I guess that's a start."

Alex tilted her head and ran her fingers through his hair. "A start?"

Nico grinned and nodded. "A start to you making it up to me."

Alex laughed and rolled over towards Nico to straddle him. "Yeah…yeah maybe it is." She grinned and leaned down to press a soft kiss to Nico's nose. "But first…could you drop me off at work?"

Nico sat up straighter, a slight frown on his handsome features. "Work? The photo shoot thing?"

Alex smiled and nodded. "Yup!" her hands cupped his handsome face, thumbs brushing over his browned features. "I am going to talk to Mr. Carlyle about a few things."

"Like what?" Nico grinned and tilted his head slightly to press a soft kiss to Alex's wrist.

"Like how I can't be his make out buddy anymore." She giggled and pressed another kiss to Nico's nose. "And like how I need a full time chauffeur and guide?"

She squeaked as Nico lunged forwards, playfully nipping at her throat. "Oh you want to boss me around now eh?"

She laughed softly as he continued to nip teasing, tickling kisses along her neck and jaw line. "Maybe?" she arched a brow playfully at him. "But I have to warn you, as your employer I WILL demand on the spot make out sessions without question!"

Nico laughed softly and leaned forward to kiss Alex. "Whatever you say boss lady!"

Alex grinned softly and wrapped her arms around Nico's neck, pulling him back down against her. She still had a full month's contract to fulfill and she was going to work her ass off every single day of it, but today, today she was going to take a personal day.

THE END

Keep reading for a
Sneak Preview of
"COMIC CON LOVE",
Book 3
in
Alexandra's
LOVE & ROMANCE
Series.

Denise Daniella Darcy

Sneak Preview of *COMIC CON LOVE*, Book 3

Chapter 1 -- Making plans

"San Diego?" Alex looked up from the bed where she was comfortably sprawled wearing her favorite 'snuggly' shorts, one hand buried in a super-sized bucket of popcorn. "Why are you going to San Diego?"

The question was directed towards the open door of Gabby's closet, the depth of which seemed to be the equivalent of a separate room altogether. "Comic Con," Gabby replied as she walked out of the closet carrying a hefty load of clothes in her arms which she promptly dumped on the bed, partly burying Alex under it.

Alex had been helping Gabby move into her new apartment over the course of the last month. It was the first apartment that Gabby had gotten on her own without the help of current or ex-boyfriends or without the aid of male admirers of any ilk. It was a significant change for her, but it was just one of many that Gabby had made in her life. The first of which was to patch things up with Alex.

She had been the first one to receive Alex when she returned from Hawaii and even though Alex had been ready to patch things up with Gabby for some time now it meant a great deal to her that Gabby would make the first move. She had never been the kind to do so, to say sorry, to even admit her mistake or guilt.

Ever since their school days Alex had had to learn how to maneuver around Gabby's unwillingness to see any faults of her own. It wasn't until much later that Alex had realized that all of Gabby's haughtiness, her self-centeredness, was her own means of protecting herself. She had never once thought of questioning Gabby about her various dysfunctions, perhaps because Gabby had never brought up Alex's.

It was perhaps this fact that was responsible for the depth and duration of their friendship. They complimented each other's neuroses perfectly.

"Comic Con?" Alex sat up on the bed, sending more than a few of Gabby's clothes tumbling to the floor. "Comic Con? YOU are going to Comic Con?" Alex couldn't help the incredulous smile that accompanied her words.

"Alex…just…" Gabby returned back into the closet with an exasperated grunt and moments later there was the sound of frantic rustling and boxes moving. Alex shook her head and jumped off the bed to go stand in the closet, blocking the light.

"Gabby, why are you going to Comic Con? What are you going to do there? It's all geeks and nerds and comic book fans and anime fanatics."

(Editor's Note: Anime are Japanese animated productions usually featuring hand-drawn or computer animation. The word is the abbreviated pronunciation of "animation" in Japanese, where this term references all animation. Cosplay, short for costume play, is a performance art in which participants called cosplayers wear costumes and fashion accessories to represent a specific character or idea that is usually identified with a unique name.)

Alex paused mid-sentence before her eyes widened. "Oh no! Oh Gabby don't tell me…you're cosplaying?" Alex didn't know whether to be excited or worried about the fact that her best friend would be getting into skimpy versions of character outfits and prance around a convention hall filled with anime enthusiasts.

Gabby had seated herself cross legged on the floor of her closet, Jimmy Choos and Loboutins scattered all around her in disrespectful clutter. She looked up from her make shift throne with a look that spoke of defeat and frustration and the pouty intemperance of someone who was going to have to do something she didn't want to. Alex laughed and shook her head slightly, resisting the urge to pull on those once chubby cheeks of her friend.

"You ARE going to be cosplaying aren't you?" Alex slid down to sit beside Gabby, cross legged the same as her friend. Gabby sighed softly and pouted huffily. Alex responded with a soft laugh and squeezed her friend's shoulder. "I thought you weren't into all that stuff…Gabby do you even KNOW any characters you could cosplay as?"

Gabby sneered angrily as she tossed a bunched up ball of fabric aimlessly at the wall. "Of course I don't! But you know...I have to pay the bills somehow." She huffed and slid up onto her feet with an easy grace that made Alex realize why she could wrap men around her little finger so easily. "Look, it's an easy gig, easy money, and the trip and accommodation is paid for."

Gabby paused for a moment as she leaned against the doorway of her closet, long slender fingers doodling on the wooden frame. "And...they said I could bring up to five people."

"Yeah?" Alex looked up from where she was sitting, "so like your own team of...of..." and then she realized what Gabby was hinting at.

"Oh no...oh no nono," Alex laughed nervously as she stood up, the crumpled mess of one of Gabby's shirts in one hand.

"Aww, come on!" Gabby whined. "You know I don't have anyone else to go with." Alex sputtered softly, backing away towards the back of the closet.

"Wait." Alex asked. "Don't you have like a bazillion photographers just begging to work with you?"

Gabby sighed softly. "None that will work with me for free."

Alex blinked at those words. "What? So I'm not even getting paid?"

Gabby glared momentarily at Alex before muttering slowly, her words spoken through gritted teeth. "If I had any money I wouldn't have taken this dorky gig, now would I?"

Alex laughed softly and held up her hands in front of her in surrender. "Fine! Fine! I'll go, I'll go!"

Chapter 2 -- Gathering the team

"San Diego?" Lawrence Luciano looked up from his favorite chair at the kitchen table where he had been presented with a pair of tickets by his daughter in the middle of his early morning breakfast. "Why are you going to San Diego?"

"We," Alex replied as she stirred the large, hot mug of cocoa that she had been handed by her father. "WE are going to San Diego, you, me, Cynthia, all of us." She leaned back against the kitchen counter, both hands wrapped around the warmth of the mug she was holding and sipped delicately from the heated liquid as she waited for her father to finish his questions.

"What's a 'Comic Con'? Is that like a comedian's convention or something?" He put the glossy black tickets down on the table, rough, calloused fingers caressing the smooth surface of the stubs lazily. Alex had to smile at her father, he was the smartest, most intelligent man she knew but sometimes he sounded like someone straight out of the nineteen forties.

"No Dad, it's not a comedian's convention, it's sort of like...um," Alex pondered over the words, her gaze wandering up over the far wall of the kitchen. "Remember when I was in high school, a few of my friends would come over and bring their comic books and all the really cool stuff over and we would trade and read and just hang out?"

Lawrence raised an eyebrow over the thick rim of his glasses, the hint of a playful smile flirting on his lips. "'Really cool stuff'?"

Alex ignored the bait of his tone and continued straight on. "Well, it's kind of like that except there are hundreds and hundreds of people doing it in the open and none of them are going to get wedgies or swirlies later on."

Lawrence laughed softly, his fingers deftly plucked the stem of his glasses from behind his ear to place them down on the table over the tickets. "Sounds like fun," he said, smiling up at Alex. "But I still don't get what Cynthia and I are supposed to do there?" Alex sipped delicately on the hot cocoa. It was one of the many constants that she could count on whenever she came over to her father's. Cocoa and questions.

"You don't have to do anything Dad," Alex replied. "The accommodation and travel is free, you and Cynthia can go sightseeing or whatever, and Gabby and I can work." Lawrence sipped his coffee silently and raised his glance up at his daughter. Alex sighed and rolled her eyes. "It's not like that pops, we really are going to be working, well she is going to be working, I am going to be freelancing." She smiled and stirred the spoon in her cocoa. "Emphasis on the free," she said wryly.

Lawrence's glance held steady with her daughter's before he sighed softly and leaned back in his chair a little. "Darling, you know that I love you more than anything in the world, right?" His words were tinged with a combination of affection, wisdom and seriousness that only fathers could get right. "And as far as I'm concerned Gabby is as much a part of this family as you are."

Alex smiled softly at his words and added in for him, "But…?"

"But," he smiled helplessly, "I can't help but feel that sometimes you let her overshadow you a little too much."

Alex looked down at the dark liquid swirling in her mug and then back at her father, a smile on her lips. "You're right" she said quietly, "I do…sometimes, but…"

she added immediately, "this isn't one of those times, I promise."

Lawrence said nothing as he crossed his arms across his chest. He had a way of doing that which made him seem more open rather than closed off. Alex leaned back on the counter, her back supported against the cabinets that hung behind her. "I don't know pops, she is different, and she's trying to change, trying real hard. Did I tell you she got her own place? No boyfriends or anything."

Lawrence's brow arched lightly at that bit of news. "And this gig?" he asked. "No boyfriends or anything?"

Alex laughed softly. "I really don't think Gabby is going to be looking for a boyfriend in a crowd of Anime fans and comic book geeks, Dad."

Lawrence smiled and stood up from the table, a folded newspaper in one hand

and his empty cup in the other. "Ever since I have known you two," he affectionately rapped Alex on the knee with the newspaper, "Gabby and you have always been each other's strengths and I am really glad that you are doing this for her." He kissed his daughter on the forehead as he spoke. "Just make sure you get us booked for the spa treatment too, kiddo."

Alex laughed softly at his words. "So you're coming?" she hopped of the counter and took the empty cup from him, putting it in the sink to wash up later.

"Are you kidding?" he said happily. "Gabby in the midst of all those geeks? Wouldn't miss it for the world!"

Get your own copy now of "COMIC CON LOVE" to continue reading about Alexandra's adventures in love.

Dear Reader,

We hope you enjoyed this adventure-in-love story.

Make sure you don't miss out on new and exciting stories by our romance writer Triple D. Join our Preferred Customer list to stay in touch. You will get:

1. *Advance notice of new stories in the series*
2. *Special deals for preferred customers only*
3. *Flash news*

Click here to sign up now:

NEWSLETTER

And everything is FREE!

Cheers,

Sally Carruthers, *Triple D's Helper*

Candid Love

Also by Denise Daniella Darcy

Samantha's

LOVE & ROMANCE Series

First Love – Book 1

Rebound Love Book 2

Cowboy Love – Book 3

Casual Love – Book 4

Denise Daniella Darcy

Also by Denise Daniella Darcy

Alexandra's
LOVE & ROMANCE Series

Risky Love – Book 1

Candid Love Book 2

Comic Con Love – Book 3

Special Love – Book 4

Hi Readers, Denise here. I am busy writing more stories about Alexandra's adventures in love so check my website www.DeniseDaniellaDarcy.com for the most up-to-date list. Happy reading! *DDD*

Denise Daniella Darcy

Recommended Reads

If you liked *COMIC CON LOVE*, check out these other great stories by popular authors.

Not Quite Dating (Not Quite series), Catherine Bybee

Tempting Her Best Friend (A What Happens in Vegas Novel), Gina Maxwell

Night Moves, Nora Roberts

Melt For Him (a Fighting Fire novel), Lauren Blakely

Midnight Betrayal, Melinda Leigh

Denise Daniella Darcy

Denise Daniella Darcy, or Triple D as she is affectionately called by family, friends and fans, started life as a mortician's helper. Faced with the daily task of making the dead appear happy, she decided to switch careers and apply her talents to making the living happy instead. She achieves that through her Love & Romance novels. She writes from the heart, with a viewpoint that to grow you need to push your boundaries and you find happiness wherever it may appear and in any shape that it comes.

Triple D writes stimulating contemporary romances with passion, humor and a down to earth feel that resonates with her readers. She creates the 'I can't put the book down, just 1 more page before I turn out the lights' stories that keep you interested, engaged and involved.

Candid Love

Denise lives a vibrant and enthusiastic life on the west coast with a full house, including her children, cats and dogs, assorted critters, and her own personal hunk of a husband. The coffee is always on, the table always full of family and friends, and a spirited discussion is underway. And when evening rolls around, often enough a party is sent out to raid the wine cellar. Lively, fun and full of life.

Her Love and Romance novels include FIRST LOVE, REBOUND LOVE, COWBOY LOVE and CASUAL LOVE in the Samantha Series, as well as RISKY LOVE, CANDID LOVE, COMIC CON LOVE and SPECIAL LOVE in the Alexandra Series. In addition Triple D is busy writing a new series in the same romance genre featuring newcomer Charlotte.

To receive an email when Triple D releases a new novel, get on our FREE newsletter here: NEWSLETTER.

And I know she'd love you to visit her at www.DeniseDaniellaDarcy.com.

Dear Reader,

One final note. Thank you so much for reading this story. I hope you really liked it.

As you probably know, many people look at the reviews on Amazon before they decide to purchase a book.

If you liked the book, could you please take a minute to leave a 4 or 5 star review with your feedback?

You can do that right here:

<u>Amazon Review</u>

60 seconds is all I am asking you for, and it would mean the world to me. Your friendly support will certainly help me in further research & writing.

Thank you so much, and here's to happy reading.

Denise Daniella Darcy

'Triple D' to my friends

PS. Don't forget to get your
FREE ALTERNATE ENDING
here:

<u>*http://www.denisedaniellada*</u>
<u>*rcy.com/CandidLoveAltEnding*</u>

*Just my way of giving you
something extra and thanking you for
reading my books.*

*And if you have a friend who
might like my novels, perhaps you
could send her a link? As an indie
writer I need friends to make any
progress against the big guys.*

www.ingramcontent.com/pod-product-compliance
Lightning Source LLC
Chambersburg PA
CBHW060634130626
46555CB00002B/794